W9-AQN-563

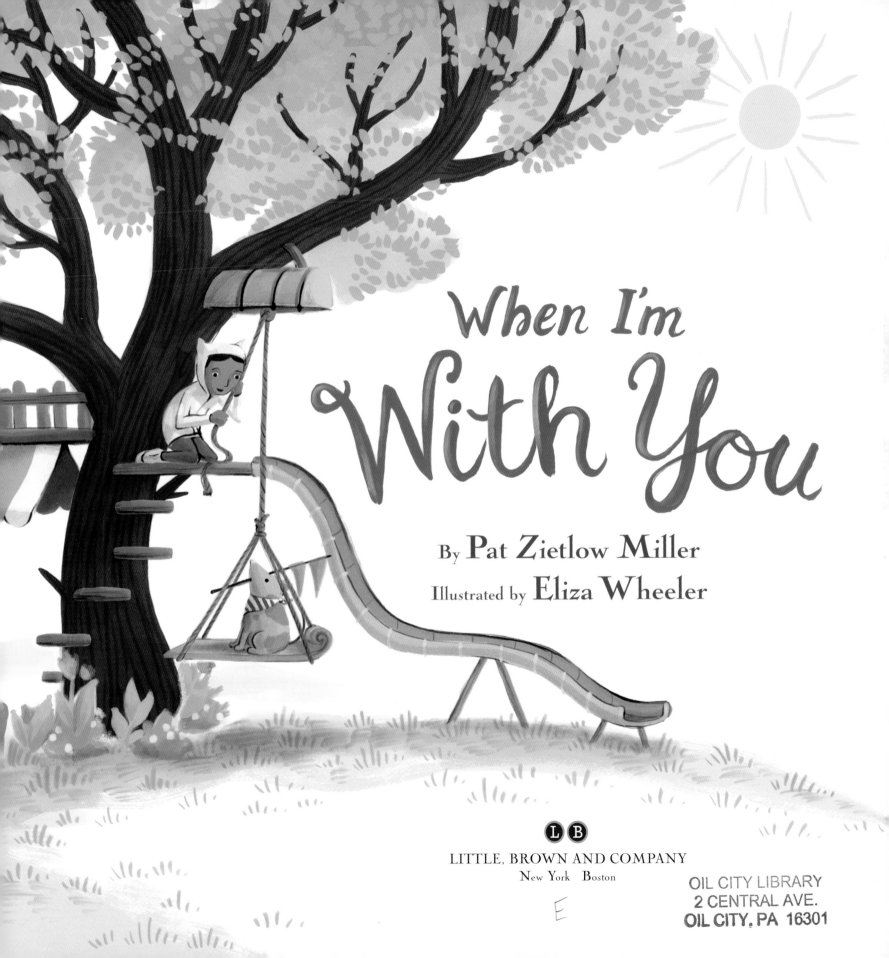

When I'm With You

By **Pat Zietlow Miller**

Illustrated by **Eliza Wheeler**

LB

LITTLE, BROWN AND COMPANY
New York   Boston

OIL CITY LIBRARY
2 CENTRAL AVE.
OIL CITY, PA 16301

E

To Ammi-Joan Paquette: It's fun making books with you —PZM

For Maddelyn—because this all started with you —EW

ABOUT THIS BOOK

The art for this book was created using ink, watercolors, acrylic paint, wax pastels, and digital collage. This book was edited by Deirdre Jones and designed by Patrick Collins with art direction from Saho Fujii. The production was supervised by Virginia Lawther, and the production editor was Annie McDonnell. The text was set in Nicolas Cochin, and the display type is hand-lettered.

Text copyright © 2022 by Pat Zietlow Miller • Illustrations copyright © 2022 by Eliza Wheeler • Cover illustration copyright © 2022 by Eliza Wheeler • Cover design by Patrick Collins • Cover copyright © 2022 by Hachette Book Group, Inc. • Hachette Book Group supports the right to free expression and the value of copyright. The purpose of copyright is to encourage writers and artists to produce the creative works that enrich our culture. • The scanning, uploading, and distribution of this book without permission is a theft of the author's intellectual property. If you would like permission to use material from the book (other than for review purposes), please contact permissions@hbgusa.com. Thank you for your support of the author's rights. • Little, Brown and Company • Hachette Book Group • 1290 Avenue of the Americas, New York, NY 10104 • Visit us at LBYR.com • First Edition: March 2022 • Little, Brown and Company is a division of Hachette Book Group, Inc. • The Little, Brown name and logo are trademarks of Hachette Book Group, Inc. • The publisher is not responsible for websites (or their content) that are not owned by the publisher. • Library of Congress Cataloging-in-Publication Data • Names: Miller, Pat Zietlow, author. | Wheeler, Eliza, illustrator. • Title: When I'm with you / by Pat Zietlow Miller ; illustrated by Eliza Wheeler. • Other titles: When I am with you • Description: First edition. | New York : Little, Brown and Company, 2022. | Audience: Ages 4–8. | Summary: Illustrations and easy-to-read, rhyming text celebrate a close friendship that has already existed for a while and is expected to last until time is through. • Identifiers: LCCN 2020050975 | ISBN 9780316429153 (hardcover) • Subjects: CYAC: Stories in rhyme. | Friendship—Fiction. • Classification: LCC PZ8.3.M6183 Wf 2022 | DDC [E]—dc23 • LC record available at https://lccn.loc.gov/2020050975 • ISBN 978-0-316-42915-3 • PRINTED IN CHINA • 1010 • 10 9 8 7 6 5 4 3 2 1

There's something that I've noticed.
Perhaps you've seen it, too....

Life is so much better
when it's me and you.

It seems I've always liked you
ever since I can recall.
I think it must have started
when we both were small.

Or maybe it came later,
once we had a chance to grow.
I really can't remember.
But this is what I know....

You're the apple on my tree.
You're the honey to my bee.
It doesn't matter what we do.

I am happier with you.

You're the numbers in my set,
all the sums I don't know yet.
But if one plus one makes two,

I'm the one who goes with you.

You're the colors that I choose
and that paint I always use.
You like pink, and I like blue.

I'll make lavender with you.

You're the hat that fits my head.
You're the hilltop for my sled.

When I sneeze,
you say, "Ah-CHOO!"
And that makes me
laugh with you.

But...
some days aren't as funny.
Skies are cloudy.
Clouds are gray.

And although
you're right beside me,
we don't have a lot to say.

You don't always do the right thing.
But I know you always try.

You help out when life gets messy.
And that's just one reason why…

You're the soap that scrubs my dish.
You're the flakes that feed my fish.
When there's lots of work to do,

it's more fun when I'm with you.

You're the basket on my bike
and the canteen for my hike.
Somewhere old or somewhere new,

I'd go anywhere with you.

Someday we'll both be older.
Doesn't that seem rather strange?
And, of course, life will be different,
but I hope we'll never change.

We might live close together...

...or be many miles apart.

But I'll find a way to keep you
in my head and in my heart.

You'll be the story that I need,
all the news that I can read.

I'll learn what, where, when, and who.
Then I'll share it all with you.

You'll be the music I will sing,
the first doorbell I will ring.
And even if we're ninety-two,

I will harmonize with you.

You'll be the key to my lock.
The right shoe for my sock.

My swing set in the park.
My flashlight in the dark.

The candle for my cake.
My favorite wish to make.

And from now till time is through…

...I will still be friends with you.

MULTIPLE-CHOICE & ESSAY QUESTIONS WITH REVIEW MATERIAL IN PREPARATION FOR THE AP UNITED STATES HISTORY EXAMINATION

(SIXTH EDITION)

Tom Barnes

D&S MARKETING SYSTEMS, INC.
1205 38th Street Brooklyn, NY 11218

w w w . d s m a r k e t i n g . c o m

ISBN # : 978-1-934780-32-9 / 1-934780-32-4

Copyright © 2014 by D&S Marketing Systems, Inc.

All rights reserved.

No part of this book may be reproduced or transmitted in any form or by any means, electronic or mechanical, including photocopying and recording, or by any information storage or retrieval system, without written permission from the publisher.

Printed in the U.S.A.